Keiko Kasza

The Pigs' Picnic

PUFFIN BOOKS

PUFFIN BOOKS
Published by the Penguin Group
Penguin Putnam Books for Young Readers, 345 Hudson Street, New York, New York 10014, U.S.A.
Penguin Books Ltd, 27 Wrights Lane, London W8 5TZ, England
Penguin Books Australia Ltd, Ringwood, Victoria, Australia
Penguin Books Canada Ltd, 10 Alcorn Avenue, Toronto, Ontario, Canada M4V 3B2
Penguin Books (N.Z.) Ltd, 182-190 Wairau Road, Auckland 10, New Zealand

Penguin Books Ltd, Registered Offices: Harmondsworth, Middlesex, England

First published in the United States of America by G. P. Putnam's Sons, 1988
Published by Puffin Books, a division of Penguin Putnam Books for Young Readers, 2001

1 3 5 7 9 10 8 6 4 2

THE LIBRARY OF CONGRESS HAS CATALOGED THE G. P. PUTNAM'S SONS EDITION AS FOLLOWS:
Kasza, Keiko
The pigs' picnic / Keiko Kasza
p. cm.
Summary: Mr. Pig, on his way to call on Miss Pig, allows his animal friends to persuade him to
don various handsome portions of their own bodies, with an alarming result.
ISBN 0-399-21543-3
[1. Pigs—Fiction. 2. Animals—Fiction. 3. Identity—Fiction.] I. Title.
PZ7.K15645Pi 1988 [E]—dc19 87-22691 CIP AC

Puffin Books ISBN 0-698-11902-9

Printed in the United States of America

To Edward Kosuke Kasza

It was a perfect day for a picnic. Mr. Pig tried to look his best. He was going to ask Miss Pig to go on a picnic with him.

"Gee, I hope she says 'yes,'" thought Mr. Pig. But he was worried, so he took a flower to impress her.

On the way to Miss Pig's house, he met
his friend the Fox. When the Fox heard
about the picnic, he said, "Let me give
you some advice, Mr. Pig. Borrow my
beautiful tail."

"There, you see how foxy you look?
Miss Pig will like that," said the Fox.
Mr. Pig was pleased.

Then he met his friend the Lion. When
the Lion heard about the picnic, he said,
"Let me give you some advice, Mr. Pig.
Borrow my beautiful hair."

"There, you see how courageous you look? Miss Pig will like that," said the Lion. Mr. Pig was pleased.

Then he met his friend the Zebra. When
the Zebra heard about the picnic, he said,
"Let me give you some advice, Mr. Pig.
Borrow my beautiful stripes."

"There, you see how handsome you look?
Miss Pig will like that," said the Zebra.
Mr. Pig was pleased. He had never felt so
handsome.

He finally arrived at Miss Pig's house and knocked on the door.

"Will you go on a picnic with me?"
he asked.

Miss Pig was shocked. "Oh, no!"
she said. "Who is this monster? If
you don't go away, I'll call Mr. Pig.
He will take care of you."

Mr. Pig ran back the way he came.
He returned the tail to the Fox, the hair
to the Lion, and the stripes to the Zebra.

And then he hurried back to Miss Pig's house, and once more he knocked on the door.

"Will you go on a picnic with me?" he asked again.

"Oh, Mr. Pig!" she cried. "I'm so glad to see you. Just now there was an ugly monster right here in this yard. I'd love to go on a picnic with you, Mr. Pig."

All the way to the picnic, Miss Pig
talked about the monster who had
visited her house. Her handsome friend
Mr. Pig listened sympathetically.

It was a perfect day for a picnic.